That's the Story of My Life

Stephanie R. Bridges

"That's the Story of My Life"

In Spirt Power and Truth Publishing, LLC Columbus, OH

For Tracey

Acknowledgements

A special thanks goes out to the amazing artist, Deborah Danzy. Thank you so much for allowing me to utilize your one of a kind painting for my book cover. Your work is amazing and should be seen and shared around the world.

My gratitude goes to the Greater Columbus Arts Council for their continued commitment to the literary arts and making sure ideas, concepts and stories manifest into publications shared with a greater audience.

Thank you to the people who allowed me to share a part of their life story, use their name or art to bring fictional and non-fictional characters to life.

A special appreciation goes to Beatrice Bridges for being the best mother an author could dream.

Finally, Thank you, Jesus! Hey Glory!

Contents

Musketeer Down

Imani fell down in the middle of on-coming traffic. It screeched its collective breaks and swerved, colliding to create a near death experience. Her body was suddenly lifted from the pavement and her legs set back into full motion with her friends, Nia and Kenzie, on either side holding her arms. They were all faded. Nia was screaming in horror over all the commotion they had caused, and the man coming towards them with fist raised and expletives flying, made it even worse. Kenzie was laughing uncontrollably, trying not to full pee her pants at the thought of death defyingly running across the street and then realizing that Imani was no longer in their midst. When she turned all she saw was Imani down with one finger held up, signaling, *wait* to the girls and *excuse me* to the traffic.

Now, they were literally running for dear life because the crazed man would not cease from the chase. Nia's life flashed before her eyes; she knew it was coming to an end. Kenzie's knife flashed before her eyes as she began to feel for the weapon she always carried on her. And Imani was blacked out, body in motion without thought or recognition of what the hell was going on or about to occur.

Damn, don't this MF got car insurance? Kenzie thought as she dug in her pocket. The knife was nowhere to be found. Imani's head jerked back, and Nia screamed. The lunatic tackled what he thought would be Imani, but his leap fell short and he ended up tussling on the ground with a braided wig. Kenzie full peed her pants. They continued running until they reached the steps inside Imani's building. It was a long four flights up.

"Let's go down," Kenzie ordered. There were only a few steps that led to a locked door barely out of site of the front entry. Imani slumped in the corner, Nia whimpered, and Kenzie held one hand over Nia's mouth and the other hand continued patting every pocket for the knife.

"You, Black rats are dead now!" the voice echoed with a thousand demons. The cement steps clapped back as he stomped his way upward.

"Let's go!" Kenzie demanded. Imani remained slumped. Nia ran out the front door. Kenzie ran up the stairs and tackled the man from behind. He lost his balanced, and gun shots rang out in the narrow stairwell, ricocheting from the walls. Now, Kenzie was afraid. She had no idea he had a gun. Imani stirred from the loud noise and stood abruptly. She made her way around the curve. She saw Nia standing with the door held wide and ran past her up the stairs towards the shots, *towards her home.* A man was facing her with a gun and a girl was on his back. *Oh, God. Is that Kenzie?*

"You're dead now," he gasped with Kenzie's arms clasped tightly around his neck in a cholkhold. The shot rang out, and Imani fell. The man tripped over her body and Kenzie let go as he careened head first into the cement block wall.

Nia let go of the open door and all hope. Losing the light from the doorway, she headed up in the darkness, passed the man's body and heard Kenzie imploring through sniffles, "Imani, get up. Please, please get up." Nia slowed her pace even more and sat on the step next to where Imani fell. Now, she had to be composed. She felt for Imani's head. It was intact, and she was still breathing.

"Kenzie, stop crying and help me lift her." Apartment doors creaked open and they heard voices. With their heads lowered, they started down the flight of stairs, and high stepped over the man's body. This time, each girl had one of Imani's arms *and* legs in tow. One more flight until they were out the building. What started as swift movement, slowed to a brisk pace as people braved the hallway. Nia pushed open the front door, and they emerged to police sirens coming from both directions. Kenzie and Nia slowly dropped Imani's legs as they simultaneously, looked for the wound and tried to look natural. "You, okay, Imani?" Nia whispered. Kenzie couldn't stop crying. Imanis legs dragged the ground and then, after a few paces, matched their stride. She started running, and so did they.

The next day, Imani's building was surrounded by yellow tape. She walked the stairs to her unit and put the key in the knob. Before she could change her mind, the door opened, and she was staring into the face of the police.

"Oh, excuse me young lady." The officer stood to the side allowing Imani room to walk in.

"Imani!" the room erupted.

"Oh, baby!" her mom called out. "Where have you been? Why didn't you call?"

"Thank you, Officer." Imani's Dad ended the celebration abruptly. "You've been a great deal of help," he continued, as he gestured to the safe return of their daughter and simultaneously, held the door open for the policeman to leave for the second time.

The officer descended the steps, slightly confused because he had come to ask questions, not assist in the search of their daughter. Apt. 4C was the last stop, and as usual with this community, no one had seen or heard a thing. All they had was Jason was seen chasing the Migos on Halloween. There had been a car pile up, but they could not link him to any of the vehicles. *He must have just witnessed the incident – a concerned citizen who allowed mounting frustrations to take over his best judgement.* The officer scratched his head again in bewilderment.The death would be written up as an accident. There was no real proof that he had chased anyone, including the Migos, that far or that he was even the same Jason, which was a favorite mask on beggars night. Besides, there were always creepy men perusing the area looking for drugs or sex. They would never know who Jason was trying to shoot or why. No matter how many eye-witnesses there were, no one had seen or heard a thing.

Imani went into her room, fell to her knees and thanked God they hadn't been killed. They made a pact to show up to school the next day as if nothing had happened. Imani heard her door and looked up from her prayer and saw her Dad in the doorway. "You do know *nothing* is ever their fault?"

"Yes, Sir. I know."

"And no more listening to all that rap music. I told y'all bout that hallow bright, scary night shit. Dressing like the damn Three Blind M…Musketeer…Amigos." Imani's father took a deep breath. "Love you," he ended softly.

"Amen," Imani whispered, responding to her father's enduring affection and ending her prayer to her Lord and Savior, "and Amen."

Crayons

No matter the shade, no matter the hue
Crayons are so much fun
I broke a couple
Tore the paper off two
And chewed a part of one
They outline, draw, color and shade
Every tone I could every dream
But when I close my eyes, the colors fade
And all the same, crayons seem
Wax form wrapped in paper
Placed in a box to share
No matter the shade, no matter the hue
Color your world with care

Tea Is Better for You

The teapot whistled, waking Brian from his sleep. *Ah, tea in the morning.* He needed a jolt to wake up, and if he drank tea and coffee he would be running to the bathroom all day. Brian's wife said tea was better for him, so he would take the cup, kiss her goodbye and head to the drive thru for coffee.

On his way to the office, Brian pondered the heaviness in the air. There wasn't a storm on the horizon – just a grey day, like the ones before it and the ones to come. Maybe it wasn't the day. Perhaps the grey cloud hovered just inside Brian's mind like the memories he couldn't release.

"Oh, Brian, it's your turn to read," the teacher announced.

Brian took a deep breath, "D-d-d-d o-o-o-gz arrrrraaaahh m-m-m-aaaanz b-b-b-esst friend!" he exhaled, as the class roared with laughter. Brian jumped from his seat and rushed toward the teacher's desk to request a hall pass. On the way, Craig, stuck out his foot, and Brian fell to the floor. The sudden collision released his bladder.

"Eeww! Gross!" was all he could hear as he lie on the white tiled floor - frozen in time.

Brian reached for his briefcase in the backseat and headed inside the building where he worked for the past eight years. He had moved up in the organization securing a position in management. He liked his job; his colleagues were great. But anytime he heard people talking and laughing outside his office, he knew they were making fun of him.

The same week as the "accident" in class, the pale girl with mousy brown mushroom hair, caught up with Brian on the walk home. "They're all jerks. There's nothing wrong with stuttering," she spat through braces and a lisp. Kelly was a close 2nd to Brian on the list of kids to bully. He couldn't fathom how the two of them together would help matters. So, he ignored her, quickened his pace, and abruptly turned to cross the street.

"Hey, wait! Do you want to go to the danceth?" Kelly's voice strained to reach a pitch, Brian, had never witnessed. The sound stopped him in his tracks. He turned, looked at Kelly and couldn't pick out one thing he liked about her. He even enjoyed her turns at being tormented because it meant he got a break.

"Sure!" he yelled back and jumped out of the street just in time to miss on-coming traffic.

Brian was tripped twice on the dance floor, but the 2nd time he kept his balance. Kelly was shoved into the punch, it wobbled spilling onto her dress, but Brian grabbed her arm before she crashed completely into the table. Craig got on the mic and dedicated a song stuttering every syllable, but hardly anyone laughed. And kids threw wadded up paper at Kelly that read "Most Likely to be Ugly," but she didn't bother to pick them up and read them. It was a successful night.

Kelly was now a convincing Malaysian Straight 100% Human Hair Brunette, the braces were gone, her skin was sun kissed by Maybelline personally and she only lisped occasionally at Brian's request. Brian stopped stuttering his senior year of high school, and they got married after college. Kelly never once mentioned the day that Brian peed his pants in class on the floor in front of everyone. But every morning, she offered him tea.

The Best Night of Taylor's Life

Taylor sat still while her makeup was being applied. She felt like a real celebrity. Hair, wardrobe, makeup, mani/pedi you name it; she was being primped and pampered for what would be the best night of her life. Prom. Her dress was still hanging on the door. She admired the sequined bodice that flared into a beautiful ball gown. It was sunshine yellow. Taylor scanned her closet and saw nothing yellow. Her eyes perused the floor that had as many clothes strewn across it, as were hung. One lemon tank top that she never wore peeked out from the corner. Taylor looked horrible in yellow. But after trying on at least thirty dresses, at what felt like as many stores, this was *the one*. Well, the only affordable one. There were other dresses, but before she could reach out and brush her hand against the boning of their frame, her mother had the tag in her grasp and announced "No, this is not a dress for someone with a baby." Taylor heard that every day of her pregnancy and into the first 5 months of her daughter, Drema's life. *No, that makeup, salon, shoe, clutch, limo, lip gloss, hair moisturizer, toothpaste, cereal is not for someone with a baby.* Taylor was amazed that her mother could make the same statement, with the same inflection, and maintain the same grave intent without breaking into laughter. She and her twin sister, Abby, stood out of their mother's sight and mimicked her words.

"What's funny?" her mother's voice raised like a hand ready to swat.

"Nothing, Momma." Both girls assured as Taylor pulled her to the clearance rack with the yellow dress.

Abby did Taylor's nape length hair with a small flat iron that pressed through thin wefts. The two girls went to the drug store the night before and purchased a manicure and pedicure system. They stayed up all night doing their nails and toes, laughing about prom shopping, practicing dance moves and attending to Taylor's baby, Drema. Makeup was the finishing step and Taylor's cousin, Brandi, did it for free. They would take her boyfriend/baby daddy, Jasper's car. Taylor looked at her phone, it was 6:30 PM. Prom started at 7:30 PM. She reviewed everything she still needed to do before the official kick off to the best night of her life. Finish makeup, put dress and shoes on, feed baby, put her to sleep. The knock on the door would come soon and Taylor could feel her scalp tingle in preparation for a full-blown flop sweat. But before she could panic, her spinning mind was interrupted.

"Oh, Taylor, you look stunning," Brandi crooned. "Wait!" she grabbed her shoulders to stop her from turning to the mirror. "Don't look until you put on your dress." Brandi's sentiments were nuanced with the magic of make-believe.

"Okay!" Taylor's exuberance interrupted the surreal, and she jumped out the chair and did a high knee, half jog, half jump step with excitement. She grabbed the dress hanging on the door and headed to the bathroom, but the door was shut and she could see the light coming from underneath - occupied. Taylor stayed in the hallway. There was just enough space and Taylor thought she may have even felt a breeze. She took off her grey sweats and black tank top. Brandi walked into the hallway and put a towel over her head to protect her pixie hairdo and safeguard the ball gown from her painted guise.

"Lift your arms straight up." Brandi insisted. Brandi got the dress over her arms and began to pull from the bottom. Taylor squirmed back and forth, side to side until her face was free, then arms. While Brandi pulled, Taylor pushed down from the top until the gown was in place. Both ladies took a deep breath.

Taylor spun around, "Zip me!" *If only it was that easy*. The gulf was wide. Brandi said a prayer under her breadth.

When the zipper finally reached the top, Brandi called out, "Won't He do it?"

"Yes, He will," Taylor responded.

"Hey Glory!" The girls went into a mini-church shout.

Drema must have known her mother was ready, because right before Brandi could guide Taylor's foot into the left shoe, they heard a small cry.

"These shoes are the bomb, Girl." Brandi spoke while still admiring the rhinestone studded heels. All her accoutrement was on point, but the shoes were designer, and probably cost more than everything else put together.

"Yes, aren't they nice? They're Abby's from last year's prom. I love them." Taylor responded matter-of-factly.

"Okay, now look." Brandi turned Taylor around to the full-length mirror that leaned against the wall. "I'll go get the baby."

Taylor looked in the mirror and she almost couldn't believe her own eyes. She looked like a princess. "I'm a princess." She repeatedly affirmed.

Brandi had the baby in her arms and tears in her eyes. "Yes, you are a princess. But girl, I gotta go." She put the burping towel over Taylor's shoulder and handed her Drema. Brandi loved her little cousin, but she wasn't real big on babies. They made her nervous. They gave each other air kisses and Brandi let herself out.

"Okay, clutch, lipstick, cash, door key…" Taylor said each word in an animated voice as if she were telling Drema a fairytale as she dropped each item in the satin clutch. She started for the stairs and then turned "Oh, shawl. That's right my little snugum wugum, shawl." She repeated in a sing-songy voice.

Brandi walked slowly down the staircase, careful not to drop shawl, bag or baby. If she tripped in the designer stilettos, that she was not accustomed to wearing, all would be lost. So, she called on the name of Jesus grateful for each step. Taylor put Drema in her play seat and went to the kitchen to warm a bottle of breast milk. It took three days for Taylor to pump and properly store enough milk for this evening. Before she sat down to feed Drema she looked out the window. No passing cars. She grabbed her clutch to look at her phone and check the time. *Ugh!* She realized she left her phone upstairs. She took a deep breath and fed Drema. She anticipated a knock on the door any moment. Drema was fed, burped and rocked back to sleep and still Taylor did not hear any music outside, a car pull up or a knock at the door. It was 7:30 pm. Her phone rang, and her heart sank. She did not want to chance the steps again in stilettos nor did she feel the urgency to kick off her heals and make a run for it. There wasn't anyone she wanted to speak to on the phone. As soon as Taylor's cell stopped ringing, another ring-tone began playing.

She tried not to listen but couldn't help but hear every word of the one-sided conversation. The voice feigned understanding. "Oh, no that happens. You can only do what you can do. No, she won't be mad. Thank you for at least calling. Letting us know."

Taylor stared at the steps, the same steps, she had called out to Jesus twelve times just minutes before, and a tear rolled down her face. This could not be happening. Her sister, Abby, was going to prom the 2nd year in a row; Taylor wouldn't even make one – her senior prom. Embarrassed by the tears that were no longer taking turns dropping one by one, but now puddled over her beautiful makeup, and cleared away her princess façade. Taylor turned back to the window, stared into the darkness and braced herself on the sill as she listened to the creak of all twelve steps.

"Hey, Sweetheart." The voice was warm with consolation. Taylor turned to see Jasper and her emotions mixed. He was so handsome in the black suit they found at the thrift store, and his new vest and bowtie looked like a splash of sunshine straight from Taylor's dress. Jasper took Taylor in his arms. "The baby sitter canceled."

Jasper and Taylor listened to music, exchanged corsage and boutonniere, took selfies, ate peanut butter crackers, drank tap water on ice and did all the dances that Taylor had been practicing. Drema drank the breast milk her mother had worked so hard to express from a bottle and swayed the night away with her parents. Drema donned an expensive yellow onesie that her grandmother had purchased, before they knew the sex of the baby. *Oh, yellow, like her sunshine.*

It started to all make sense. Prom, graduation parties, going off to college, senior pictures and trips – were not for someone with a baby. At least, not in Taylor's case; only more responsibility than a teen mom and dad could possibly imagine. Her mother's words were an attempt to prepare her for all the many sacrifices that were yet to come. But Taylor was right about one thing; this was one of the best nights of her life.

Happy Anniversary

My doubts have subsided, dissipated like dust remodeled into trust.

My fears still real no longer haunt, only taunt playfully.

My insecurities once heightened are highlighted 'cause sometimes I can't help but to show off.

My isms start with A's; my phobias are afraid, dismayed by the transformation of their former host.

Let us toast to the new now me, brave in the face of Love's victory,

On this our primitive anniversary, I declare in your presence, I am petrified.

The Dandelion House

A Literary Tryptic

Part I

Dandelions are a child's first flower; abundant, brilliant, sunshine sprouting past the earth. "You can't catch me, you can't catch me," they chant in unison like the children who pick them one by one. Dandelions make up a mother's first spring bouquet, as both mother and child delight in the wonder of God's creation and first love. "Mommy, this is for you."

As the years go by and the heads of dandelion's get popped off in childhood rituals that mimic maternity and childbirth, somewhere in the midst of all the magic, the secret is shared. But not in a whisper like any respectable secret is told, no nothing hushed or considerate about its spread. "Stop picking those things, they're weeds." *Weeds*? Now, they no longer convey sunshine, spring or new births. The white wispy wishes so fun to blow through the air have turned into poisoned truths.

But how do you tell a dandelion; a little black girl birthed special by Mother Earth herself to stop emerging, stop dancing with breezy blue skies, stop being easy on sunny summer days. Quit playing, laughing, enjoying life, you ugly; a weed, unwanted with poisoned seed. Naw, the dandelion just gonna keep growing until you forced to pick it up and see the butter reflected on your chin.

Part II

I know firsthand bout sadness. In fact, me and sadness take long walks together arm and arm down winding paths through nature's ravines. When we have to be a part for more than a week or two, we write five page long love letters, the kind schoolgirl's draw hearts on to make schoolboy's blush. All written out on hand-painted stationery with endless green meadows; sans the dandelions. Chirping birds make a fit replacement. Yes, the birds sing each lyric painstakingly composed to convey - sadness and I will never part.

I'm sure we just close friends and not *real* lovers. We got separate rooms. Although, whenever she can't sleep, she come to my room and keep me up as long as she please, rustling around and stealing the covers, a few times up all night with tears streaming down her face. I do my best to comfort her, but really, I wish she'd just go back to her own room and leave me be. We break up every so often. I think the longest she staid gone was six months.

"Did you miss me?" is always her first words clamoring through the door, out of breath and perspiring like she traveled land and sea to get back to me. I just pretend I don't see, hear or even know she back - go on bout my business. But I guess in a way I do miss her. She real familiar like, and I ain't made room for nobody/nothing else.

Part III

I would like to marry an artist; a painter to be precise. Someone who specializes in abstract works but performs a miraculous feat in realism - at least once a year. So, I can be secure in the fact that his genius *is* genius. Okay, I know this is asking a lot, but someone who is appreciated, celebrated, compensated while living.

I would be his wife. Conservative in comparison - his eccentricity would over shadow my quirks. I'd be safe and keep him covered. He wouldn't ask much of me at all because the magic would reside inside his head and be interpreted through his hands. Whenever he comes out to inhale something other than paint fumes, I'd be the first one he'd see applauding his brilliance, framing and hanging his masterpieces for all to admire. He would never witness the price tags and sold stickers I brandish with delight while he's abracadabra-ing our existence. Only I would never sell the ones of me, the miraculous feats in realism.

He lives in his head, and I live just outside in a home that resembles an art gallery of historic proportions; big and modern, some fancy architectural creation. We got loyal people too, staff - folk to cook, keep the children, keep us safe from intruders, clean up. Only we can't seem to keep a gardener. They get so mad at all the weeds on the property; say it reflects badly on their craft, like they an artist or something too. But my husband *love* him some dandelions; say they his muse.

Devonte's Choice

Devonte picked up Lia every morning before heading out for school. They would walk to the bus stop together and wait in whatever elements presented themselves – wind, rain, snow, sun – everything was more bearable together. But on this day, Lia wasn't to be found. She didn't stick her head out the window and yell down, "I'm ready. Here I come!" Devonte could always tell by the inflection in her voice whether they were going to make or miss the bus. But today the window remained closed and the light in her room was off. Devonte had a cellphone, but it didn't have service.

He walked around to the front of the building and hopped the stairs two at a time all the way up to the sixth floor. Out of breath, with a light spray of perspiration, Devonte leaned his forehead against the door as he knocked.

"Who is it?" The high-pitched voice sounded disturbed by the interruption.

"Where's Lia? Let me in Lil' Guy," Devonte responded still out of breadth.

The door clicked and opened slowly revealing a stark living room with the essential matching couch, chair, coffee table and end table.

"Hey Lil' Buddy!" Devonte palmed the back of Ronrico's head and shook it back and forth."

"Hey man, STOP!" Rico was mid stride on his way to his chair with a large bowl of cereal. With each shake, the bowl wobbled, and milk and Cocoa O's splattered the floor.

Devonte flopped on the couch and watched for a moment while Scooby Doo and Scrappy ran in place. He was tempted to grab a bowl and just chill for the day too.

"My bad, Lil' Man, where's your sister?

"I don't know," Rico responded still annoyed.

Devonte grabbed the piece of paper that was on the end table. It had an address scribbled down.

Devonte's heart started pumping quicker than his mind and body could respond. He stuffed the paper in his pocket and headed out the still ajar door. "Okay, Lil' Dude, I'm out."

Rico just stared at the t.v. shoveling a huge spoon-full of Cocoa O's in his mouth.

Back outside Devonte looked around for direction, geographic and universal. He decided on the train. He ran all the way to the subway. Devonte put his earbuds in, even though he wasn't listening to anything, pulled his hat down over his eyes, and lowered his head. He prayed. It sounded just like his Grandma in his mind. But audibly he only repeated, "Please Lord, help me. Help us."

Devonte looked at the paper and then back up at the address on the sign. Every number matched. He walked up and banged too hard for it to be a normal request to enter.

"What the heck is wrong with you?" The woman at the door asked annoyed by the loud knock.

"My apologies, I'm looking for Lia. Malia Talisha Johnson," with each syllable Devonte's tone changed. He didn't know whether to be stern, humble, angry or worried to gain access.

"Sorry young man. I cannot help you."

Devonte put his hand up as a barrier to the door fully closing. "Lia. Noooo, Lia. I'm here. Come out!" His tone rang evenly with passionate concern this time.

The woman pushed back harder and the door slammed shut.

Devonte banged even harder on the door and yelled out angrily, "Malia Talisha Johnson, come out now!" Devonte sounded like a father giving a child an ultimatum. The only thing left was to count to three. The door looked solid, but the adrenaline pumped him up to slam his whole frame against the door in an attempt to burst it open. "One! Two! Thr…"

The door swung wide and a very tall slender man looked down at Devonte. "Hey son, I'm gonna have to ask you to move along. You are disturbing the peace, and this is not the place for that."

His voice was calming and almost knocked Devonte off his game. "Not without Lia." Devonte looked up to meet the Security Guard's gaze. He grabbed the hat off his head and held it to his chest, "Please, sir."

"Get out of here kid, before I have to call the police."

Police. Devonte imagined his body bleeding out, while the police and paramedics stood by chatting it up. He put his hat back on his head and stepped away from the door. He looked out again for direction, but found none. He sat on the ground in front of the building and watched as his tears smudged the numbers Lia had written on the paper. The police siren startled Devonte into a standing position, with one look back at the building he thought, *maybe Lia wasn't in there.*

Devonte's heart was racing, but he forcefully made his body move slowly, keeping his hands visible down by his side. Devonte didn't hear the door open or see the Security Guard point in his direction and say, "There he is."

Lia walked quickly to catch up and said his name repeatedly, "Devonte. Devonte. Devonte!" But he couldn't hear her over the police car siren that slowed next to him. The officers looked over at his direction and then sped off down the street.

"Devonte Emanuel Miller!" The voice sounded just like his Grandma's. Devonte turned to see Lia jogging toward him. He opened his arms to catch her as she jumped. "You came. How'd you know?"

Devonte put Lia down. "We're connected," he whispered in her ear. He took a step back and asked, "Did you go through with it?"

Devonte and Lia both put a hand on Lia's stomach. "How could I with you yelling my government all loud out here in these streets? We are having a baby."

"How about Denisha or LeVon?" Devonte asked laughing while they walked back to the train.

"*What*? How bout Elisha or Tevin?" Lia, quipped back.

Devonte spoke with compassionate concern, "Hmmm, that don't sound ghetto enough for your family." They burst out laughing because they both knew he might be right.

The Storyteller

The key to my being relies on the beat of the drum, an African rhythmic vibrato. It keeps my breadth steady and my pulse at the tip of your ebony thumb; tapping, pounding, rapping at the hide covered trunk – Thump. Thump. The sound is magical lows that reach the depth of my knowing. Resistance giving to movement, I succumb; run, dance, jump to the beat of the drum. Heart races, key in place to unlock the story of whence my Ancestors come. I sing praises to the Most High, Who created the Motherland that gave birth to her African Son; tapping, pounding, rapping his magical rhythmic drum.

Momma is that You?

Aretha rang the doorbell. She thought her family would be on the porch to greet her. The door swung wide, and all she saw was an empty hallway. Someone had to be behind the door, but Aretha felt a little creepy or maybe it was dejected. Didn't anyone care she had arrived safely after years of being away? She grabbed her bags, barely getting them through the door before they collapsed. Aretha walked in and looked behind the door.

There was a tall dark man with stark eyes. Aretha's heartbeat quickened. More young men were drinking beer, smoking weed and playing video games in the living room to the left of the foyer. Aretha saw a gun in plain sight on the coffee table.

"I'm sorry, I must have the wrong..."

"No, Auntie, you got it. It's me, Kev."

"Kevin? Lil, Kevin? Oh, my Lord," Aretha spoke with concern and relief simultaneously. She smiled broadly, and they embraced.

"Who are those people?" Aretha gestured to the smoke-filled room.

"Aw, nobody. Just my peeps."

Aretha panicked, "Where's your grandma?" She imagined her up in the attic, seated in a rocking chair, clasping a cross against her chest, with a gunshot wound to the head. Before he could respond, Aretha grabbed Kevin's arm for support from collapsing. "And your Momma, Kevin, where is she?"

Again, Aretha fathomed the worst. He wouldn't kill his own Momma, would he? Maybe she was tied up down in the cellar praying for deliverance.

"They in there, Auntie." It was Kevin's turn to gesture, and he did so with a long brisk movement that jerked Aretha's hand away and sent her in the direction of the long dark hall.

The hallway opened into the kitchen on the right. Nothing. And on the left was the dining room. Still. Nothing. She kept walking toward her least favorite "room" that was added in the seventies and hanging on by two nails and duct tape. Aretha missed the step down. Her back foot got caught, and she tumbled landing flat on the floor.

"Oh, Lawd! Po, chile," Aretha heard her Momma's voice. Her Uncle Sherman lifted her up.

"Surprise!" the room was filled with family and friends. There was takeout chicken and ribs; liquor, beer, and wine; and more smoke from weed and cigarettes. The music was turned up, and the bass dropped with rhyming expletives. A banner read, "Welcome Home, Ree Ree!" Her Momma hated that name.

Nancy rushed to her sister's side and yelled loudly over the music, "I'm sorry, Ree Ree. I tol' Momma this was too much for someone just gettin' outta prison." Aretha nodded her head still in shock. She wrenched her neck back to the kitchen. No home cooking; no crosses above the window; even the picture of white Jesus was gone. Aretha had read about cloning. She took two shots of rum and shimmied into the center of the party. Ree Ree got real cool with Kev and his peeps; but she never once ventured up to the attic or down to the cellar.

It's All the Way LIVE

The ground shook with fear under every step Jai took. She was big, brown and round everywhere right. People took notice of her beauty and her swag, but today she turned heads because of the determined look on her face to tear ish up. Damn, didn't nobody want none of that furor, but they were real curious as to who was about to get it.

What started as one, turned to three until finally a crowd had colluded to have her back or turn their back, depending on the outcome of the whoopass she was about to uncan.

"I think she's headed to Aisha's," said Stacy.

"But that's her best friend," Trina replied.

"Was her best friend. Aisha rode home with Vic yesterday."

"Flamboyant Vic?" Trina questioned with a hand flourish as she spoke.

"Well, nowadays they fluid."

"In what language?" Trina questioned.

Stacy, tilted her head, "Huh?"

"Where was Jai?" Trina continued.

"Home sick."

Trina was becoming annoyed by the story Stacy was spinning. "Homesick? She aint gone nowhere but school, *if* she go there."

"At home. She was sick," Stacy spoke slowly for the comprehensively challenged.

"Mmmm, she don't look sick."

"Morning sickness. But you aint heard it from me."

Trina's eyes got big, "Chile, you serious?"

"Serious as a Baby Momma with a MIA Baby Daddy."

"Well, I'll be." Trina shook her head, "Guess it don't matter if he fluid in Spanish, Swahili, or Sri Lankan, if he move to Miami."

Stacy and Trina were too old to follow along with the crowd of teenagers, but they never outgrew being the neighborhood gossips. Years back, soon as it was over, they would get the news, but now they could watch it all go down LIVE.

Stacy turned to the young man who was standing with them on the porch awaiting marching orders. "True, don't forget to aim the phone close enough to see, but far enough back to get all the action." True was their plug for all the play by play footage and turning fiction into fact. He would go wherever the action took him inside the neighborhood. He was a real roving reporter within a one-mile radius.

"And don't be shaking and moving so much. I aint paying you, if I can't see and hear it like I'm front row," Trina warned.

"Yeah, quit being so damn scary, True. They aint got no guns down there. Least not that I know of," Stacy added.

Stacy pulled out her cellphone and clicked on the social media app to watch the LIVE feed. So far, they couldn't see a dang thang, but the camera bumbling. Trina jumped down from the porch and caught a glimpse of True trying to push through the crowd. Finally, some action.

Jai was banging on Aisha's door. "Get out here trick! You bout to get this smoke. I don't care, pregnant or not. It's on, hoe."

"Ooooh, damn. That aint right. Your best friend and your man," the voices from the crowd instigated.

The door opened slowly, and Jai peered inside. Nobody. She felt a tug on her jacket and looked down to see Aisha's little sister, Mi`Asia. All the anger quickly flushed out of Jai's face.

"Hey, Little Momma." She bent down to pick the toddler up. "Where's your sister? What's wrong?" Jai bounced the baby on her hip, wiped the tear on her face, and closed the door behind them. But not before rolling her eyes and her neck for all her onlookers.

"Awww, damn!" Stacy and Trina spoke in unison with the disappointed crowd.

Trina jumped off the porch again. And she could see the crowd begin to disperse. A couple people sat comfortably on the porch, awaiting Jai's return, and True headed back their way. Trina had a mind not to pay him. For what? Wasn't no action.

But before Trina could get back on her porch, the real action started.

"Oh, God! Somebody help!" The door opened wide and Jai yelled out still holding the toddler. Two people, plus True ran in. Two others dialed 911, and everyone else left the scene before they could be ID'd, questioned or detained.

The visual was shaky but they could clearly see Aisha lying on the floor. Vic was down on his knees holding her limp body on his lap. "She's dead, Jai. I think she's dead."

Then the LIVE feed ended. Stacy and Trina paced back and forth on the porch, until they heard the ambulance and saw the police cars. Trina and Stacy jumped down off the porch and looked down the street. The stretcher finally came out and Aisha's body was rolled out with her face uncovered and an IV attached.

"Whew, she's alive!" Trina spoke loud enough to alert the neighborhood.

Before they could get back up on the porch, Stacy caught a glimpse of another stretcher rolling out.

"Is that, True?" Stacy questioned.

"What you calling me a liar?" Trina quipped angrily.

"No, goofy. True, the Plug, Roving Reporter, Truuuueeee. Look."

Trina squinted. "Oh, God, that is True."

Before Stacy could stop her, Trina took off running down the street. Stacy followed. It felt like they were kids again, only when they reached the scene, the ambulance doors were closing, and they couldn't catch their breath to speak. "I'm sorry ladies," the EMT responded to the worried look on their faces. "We cannot open the doors. We are taking them to Grant Hospital." They watched as the ambulance drove away.

Stacy and Trina didn't have a car and even if they did, they did not do hospitals. Instinctively, Stacy, looked down at her phone and clicked on the social media app, and wouldn't you know it, there was True reporting LIVE from inside the ambulance.

Stacy and Trina were tired after running down the street, so they made themselves comfortable on Aisha's porch and watched the LIVE feed.

It turns out no one was pregnant. The neighborhood thought Aisha was pregnant and the rumor spread to Jai. She was upset with Aisha because they promised each other since 3rd grade they wouldn't get pregnant, take drugs or do anything to mess up their plans to attend an HBCU outside the city they grew up in. It didn't really matter which one as long as they both got in together. In 8th grade, Vic learned about his friends' plan, and he vowed to make it out with them. Jai was upset because she thought Aisha had broken their promise, when all three of them were so close to attending Central State University.

True also politely explained that Vic, whose sexuality wasn't anyone's business, wasn't romantically involved with Aisha or Jai. They were all just good friends. When Jai didn't come to school, Aisha asked Vic to give her a ride to the clinic, so she could find out why she hadn't been feeling well. She didn't want Jai to know because she didn't want to get her all worked up. Jai had recently loss her cousin who was like a sister to a sudden illness.

Turns out, Aisha was dehydrated. She was an All City Athlete, top of her class academically, and she took care of her baby sister. It was their senior year, and she had overextended herself to the point of exhaustion. The clinic wanted her to stay for an IV treatment, but she had to get home to get her baby sister, Mi`Asia, off the bus.

"Well, what happened to you?" Trina demanded loudly into the phone.

Stacy rolled her eyes and typed her question into the comments.

"Oh, that," True laughed and then he grabbed his heart. He looked to the left, then to the right and got closer to the camera. "I thought Aisha was dead. I mean dead, dead. I was just about to go into a full Mary don't you weep, Martha don't you moan, blubber. All of a sudden, the girl lurched up and projectile vomited. I passed full out, and when the paramedics came, they said I had to go to the hospital too. But it feels good. Now, I am truly a roving reporter! Grant Hospital is at least six miles away."

Stacy and Trina walked back down the street towards their porch laughing and typing "Lol" in the comments. Turns out they was all jus' good kids, making big plans to do big things away from the neighborhood and the neighborhood gossips.

Identity Crisis

When I lost my identity
It was easy maneuvering through life without thin skin
I floated, and the device was good
Til that too dissipated
No longer grounded
I awakened out of this world
With no one to relate
Afraid religion wouldn't approve of the new me
I regained my identity; it pains me worse than before
Race. Gender. Drawer.
Yet. Free. Spirits. Soar.
But how do I turn my back on love?
Moses, Black Moses, Malcolm, Martin, Marcus, Mandela and More
Chose freeing over freedom
Liberating over liberation
My skin calls me black
My sex says I'm girl
My salary laugh…she poor
I wear my Identity well
It is a labor of love
Yet. Free. Spirits. Soar.

Okay, Content, Balanced and Happy

Sylvia watched intently as her husband played the piano. Her eyes were a much better gauge than her ears, when it came to Malik's performances. They all sounded great to her, but his perception was all in his grey eyes. They would light up, flash brightly and dart to and fro, if he was pleased. If he was disappointed, his eyes would glare ferociously through the keys as if it were all he could do to recall where his fingers should tap next. Tonight was a triumph! The excitement of the crowd was palatable, roses were strewn across the wooden planks of the stage; and Sylvia tried unsuccessfully to count them between the watchful glances at Malik's dancing eyes. He would be up all night. He was always up all night, but on good nights, he wanted company. On bad nights, he wanted to be alone to beseech the sun – *But why, how could you leave me so alone in all this darkness?*

Sylvia would need coffee tonight. If she dozed off, Malik would nudge her gently, "Are you sleep?" He questioned her as if they were teenagers who made a pact to stay up until dawn trolling social media, raiding the fridge, and having experimental sex.

"No, no, I'm up my love," Sylvia would reach for him, "I'm here," and kiss his countenance back to security.

Sylvia wasn't even sure Malik enjoyed performing anymore. "You know you don't owe anything to anyone. We don't need the money," she would urge.

"I know, Sylvia. Thank you for being so sweet. It's really not that bad, though. My fans give me energy. They remind me that I'm alive – a rocker with a classical shtick," Malik would laugh at his favorite motto.

Sylvia continued, "But Malik, you get so manic, and the crash is always so hard. I think the medicine is helpful."

"Look, even if I didn't perform, I wouldn't allow myself to be drugged and out of it for the rest of my days. I don't want to be pleasant. Pleasant is for luncheons. I don't eat lunch."

"I don't want you to be pleasant; I want you to be okay. Content. Balanced. Happy." Her words sounded foreign even to her as they caught in her throat and fractured the silence.

Sylvia could have sworn there was a time when Malik was happy. It was impossible that he had always been such a brooding child. *She would not have married him, would she?* They had been together nineteen years and Sylvia loved Malik more today than she had the day they exchanged vows, but she was exhausted. If he was up, he could go weeks without sleeping. He would literally write, play, practice, and perform for days on end. If he was down, his body would curl in on itself. At night, she would just wrap her form around his because she could not penetrate his being. Some nights she would cry with him; others she would swear under her breadth just audible enough for him to glean, if he ever did care to listen; but most nights, she would lie next to him awaiting marching orders. *I'm cold; it's too hot; I'm hungry; I feel sick; I can't sleep; I can't wake up.* It took time but now she understood each code. She would be up and down three or four times a night adjusting the temperature, making sandwiches, mixing cocktails, escorting him to the restroom to purge or just pee, bringing him chamomile tea to help him relax or energy drinks to help him revive.

Then out of nowhere *Malik* would show up. Sylvia would awake to the smell of coffee, orange juice, omelets and toast. Malik would bring her breakfast in bed, run her a hot bath and massage her feet with oil. "Wow, you are so beautiful in the morning. God blessed me with an angel," he would announce, as he wiped a single tear from his grey eyes to celebrate his new discovery. Sylvia and Malik would make love like adults, he would prepare her favorite meals, they'd watch obscure movies, and most of all he would be attentive. He would listen to her words, get lost in her dark brown eyes, and attend to her every whim. On rare occasions he would even go out; shopping, dancing, dinner parties, visiting family, errands, you name it.

In the beginning, Sylvia loved these days that would peak through the clouds and emerge as tangible evidence of good times and better memories. But as the years stuttered, jerked, and ground to a halt, resentment anxiously awaited its turn. *I better enjoy this while it lasts. No telling the next time he will press his body instinctively against mine, walk with me in the park, wash a dish or even brush his teeth. And why is it always when I am ready to leave, the letter written, apologies rehearsed?*

Hate was next in line, but thankfully it never got a full turn. Ten years into the marriage, Malik had a concert one evening and Sylvia watched as his stony eyes stared intently at every press of each key. The crowd was amazed, roses scattered across the wooden boards, and even Sylvia would have floated on each note if her ears were given permission to listen, but she only watched in dismay, as Malik's grey eyes bore holes into each press of each key. After the concert, Malik would only give stark one-word answers in response to Sylvia's attempts to be reassuring, "The crowd loved you. The sound was the best I've heard in a long time. Your timing was impeccable." Doors to the car, apartment, and guestroom would slam. Early in the marriage, Sylvia would try to get him to come around, but he made it painfully clear that he wanted, no needed to be alone.

"Damn! Are you stupid? Leave me the hell alone!" It was the only time Malik ever yelled at Sylvia. So, she had already decided on this particular evening, if her husband's eyes didn't jitterbug brightly off into the distance, she wouldn't say a damn thing to him either. Malik was quiet, Sylvia was silent, and all doors slammed on cue. She planned to wash and deep condition her thick, glorious dreadlocks, use the mani/pedi system that was still new in the box, marathon watch "The Real Housewives of Atlanta", and binge eat whatever sweet treats tickled her voluptuous fancy. Oh, and she had a good mind to compose a five page 'Dear John' letter.

But despite all her preparation, she sat and thought about Malik. She gave considerable thought to, Tom, the butcher at the plaza. How his eyes would light up whenever she walked in. "I need something special tonight," Sylvia would announce to the whole entire market and not just the man behind the counter.

"Why yes, Mrs. Luttrelle. I read in the paper about the concert tomorrow night, so I already have a special cut of lean roast ready. I know, Mr. Luttrelle, loves his turkey sliced thicker, so I'm going to carve that for you right now," Tom paused and added with sincerity, "Tell him I said, hello."

"Definitely, Tom, I will. Malik is always so grateful for the special attention you give to his discriminating palate," Mrs. Lutrelle lied. "I'm sure he will be with me next time I come out."

"Oh, no I understand. He is a busy, important man. Jet setting across the country, entertaining the masses. I'll see him one of these days, I'm sure."

Malik was world renown among the classical sect and that made Sylvia somewhat of a local celebrity in the small town where they lived. She thought about La'Bel, the boutique where she bought her gowns for his performances.

"Oh, Mrs. Luttrelle, I'm so glad you are here! You know we saw you in the blogs, and you were wearing a repeat. Beautiful yes, but you're kind of a big deal and represent our brand, as well," Claire, the shop owner, spoke with insistency, "I have a few dresses already pulled for you in the back - straight off the runway! Amber go get the dresses for Mrs. Luttrelle." She shooed her intern toward the stockroom.

Sylvia smiled broadly, "Yes, you're right. I am kind of a big deal." The ladies both snickered.

"And where is *Mr. Luttrelle*?" Amber chimed in a little too eager. Sylvia watched in horror as she pulled a rack of dresses that added up to way more than a few. Sylvia would pick out two or three without trying them on and be on her way.

"He's preparing for tomorrow night's show." *Malik was actually rolled up in a ball on the walk-in closet floor two shots of whiskey away from a coma.*

When Malik shopped with Sylvia, it was always a bigger, better production. He had to try an elaborate tray of twenty new meats sliced so thin that they melted in your mouth before you could chew, and then he would order a thick cut of turkey.

"How can meats be new and why can I see through them?" Malik would question Sylvia under his breath. They would chuckle - both of their eyes widening to warn the other to quit before they erupted in laughter.

The ladies at Boutique La'Bel would pull out bottles of champagne and chocolate covered strawberries just for Malik, while Sylvia modeled dresses for what seemed to her hours. As more drinks were poured, the dresses would get shorter, neck lines lower and his hands freer. It was reminiscent of the early days, when all her ensembles were deemed inappropriate for polite company. "We'll take them all! Some for the public and some for the private show," he would declare whimsically. The intern, Amber, would hang on his every word and giggle a little too much. In the spirit of competition, Sylvia would kick her leg up high, spin round, or bend low for everyone to get a sneak peek of the private show. And Mr. Lutrelle would remember to flirt with Clair a little, as well. He was always attentive to his entire audience.

Sylvia also thought about rubbing Malik's back, cheering him on to pee, or sponge bathing him when the bed sheets began to reek. *Malik hadn't changed*. It was Sylvia who had changed. She got out of the bed and walked passed the mani/pedi system still in the box, the shampoo and conditioner that guaranteed smooth and shiny, well defined tresses, the television ready to deliver ratchetness and even the bejeweled designer gown she had dazzled in just hours earlier. Downstairs, she opened the fridge and pulled out the meat still wrapped in white deli paper. She made a sandwich fit for a rocker with a classical shtick. Sylvia headed back upstairs and stopped at the guest room door and sat down. She scarfed down the sandwich and a pickle and drank a bottle of sparkling water. She burped long and loud and then listened intently for any movement behind the door.

Her last thoughts before dozing off to sleep were the early days in their marriage, when Sylvia would cuss out and fight Malik's fans, if they were too flirtatious. When she would fall asleep at the symphony, and he would assure her it was okay, "Just try to stay awake next time because the optics aren't good." Sylvia remembered how Malik defended her when his mother called her a ghetto tramp. And a tear rolled down her cheek when she recalled how he had forgiven her, when the pictures surfaced of her affair with the violinist. "He's not even first chair in the orchestra," Malik would later chide.

She longed for the man behind the drywall, who was probably just sitting wide awake waiting on the sun to promise him it was okay to rest his tired grey eyes. She would never leave, hand him one of those stupid letters, or allow hate to creep in her spirit. That night even resentment died a slow and peaceful death.

The next morning, Malik found Sylvia asleep in the hallway. He picked her up and carried her to bed. He cleared the dishes and went down to cook breakfast. Sylvia awoke to see Malik bright as the sun. She knew he would probably need a day to rest, but by the look of things this mood would probably last a full week at the very least. Sylvia learned to appreciate all of him, but this was the Malik she could show off in public. It would be a great time to visit with Tom, see the ladies at La'Bel and even spend a day with Malik's mother. She was getting older and more forgetful. *Thank God.* They could be a full hour into the visit before Malik's Mother would fully recall her disdain for his wife. Sylvia sat up and leaned against the pillows. Malik sat the tray down over her lap and handed her a glass of orange juice.

"Oh, Love, hand me my meds," Sylvia's voice was childlike. It was her turn to be bratty and spoiled. Malik brushed his hands across her enticing frame and reached over and grabbed the pill organizer that sat on Sylvia's nightstand. He opened the dispenser that read, 'Sunday', and handed her okay, content, balanced and happy.

Black Boy with Toy Gun Killed in a Society that Covets Guns

What had happened was;
Black boy got kill
Half say it unfair – he was just being
Half say it fair – he was being black
In other news, guns are still safe
Back to you, America

African Daisy

Bamazi gripped the plant and pulled at the earth. He twisted it to the left and then back to the right. The dirt shifted out of the way to respect his effort, but the foliage would not be moved. Bamazi sat down to wonder, *what next*; he could get a shovel, but his classmates had already seen him struggling to pull the plant rooted sternly in the ground. Besides, all the shovels that Mama Oduro's 3rd grade class had, were plastic. He picked up a stick and drew a shape in the small clearing his tussle with the flower had made. He wrote, *B.T. & F.M.,* inside the heart.

Bamazi jumped when he felt a hand on his shoulder. He reached for the dirt to quickly rub out the evidence.

"No, I like it," said Folake.

Bamazi looked up into eyes the color of virgin soil. Folake sat down to more closely admire Bamazi's work. She began to slowly push and pack the ground back around the daisy. It was the prettiest flower in the garden, and she did not want to see its beauty loss for a moment, when it could be preserved for many lifetimes. Bamazi got up and ran away.

Folake wasn't sure if it was out of embarrassment or if F. M. stood for someone other than her. But she continued to hum and lovingly tend the garden, as if it were the one her Mama had so meticulously planned, plotted and planted in front of their small yellow cottage. This time, Folake jumped when she felt something wet on her hand.

"Oh, I am sorry. I didn't mean to…," Bamazi started.

Folake giggled, "Oh, Bamazi, thank you!"

With renewed assurance and strength, Bamazi tilted the plastic pale and continued to slowly water the area; careful not to splash water on Folake, oversaturate the roots, or wash away his declaration of love.

The 13th

The prisoners knew they weren't ever getting out. They weren't arrested, arraigned or found guilty. They were jus' picked up and detained, and occasionally hanged for entertainment. The town kept as many prisoners as needed to fulfill their wanton desire for free labor. The prison sat jus' outside the small town – close enough to be seen in broad day light, but too obvious to be considered noteworthy. So, no one stared, cared or took notice, but for the occasional curious child. They would pull on an adult's pant leg, skirt, purse, or the sleeve of a shirt. "Paw, Maw, Stu, Grammy…, you see that?" The one in charge would move their gaze in the direction of the small pointed finger. "Oh, you mean that building? Boy, Girl, Chile, Skip…, dem jus' niggers."

Birth Days

Massa came out, wrapped his hands around Olivia's hair and pulled. She followed neck churned in an ungodly fashion. All the slaves on the plantation stopped for a moment of prayer. There was no movement besides Becka tearing through the field screaming, "No, Massa, no! Don't take my baby way, please!"

But she was afar off and by time she had reached the spot where the little girl's head was wrenched, Massa was in the shack behind the main house. The other women gathered round Becka and told her everything was gonna be alright. They was lyin' of course. But they didn't have any vocabulary beyond a lie and a truth, and this was Becka's first time experiencing something worse than her own rape.

Massa emerged and went back inside the main house for a cool glass of lemonade.

Becka and the women pushed open the door of the shack and saw Olivia rolled in a ball so many times after that first day, it seemed to be deja vu. They would wrap her in a blanket and carry her back to the slave quarters. The women would clean the girl up best they could, finding unsoiled patchwork scraps to dress any exposed part, softly brushing her long coils into two pig tails that spoke loudly; *I am a child*.

But that too was a lie. Becka wiped away tears where there were none, and said, "Hush now, chile, Mommas here," to whimpers, non-existent. In the midst of Becka's prayers, Olivia would just get up and walk out to finish her chores.

Becka didn't get dandelion bouquets, the chance to kiss booboos on scraped knees, or a warm hug after singing a lullaby. Becka tried hard to bring back the Olivia who giggled in her sleep, hummed non-stop, and hung close to the other girls, eyes shut tight, beseeching God, when Massa came out. Now, Olivia could stare the Devil down.

Becka never understood how Martha could mutter under her breadth, "Killa, killa dead," at the site of her newborn. Some said, she evil. Others said, she virtuous.

The elders say, "Naw, she just be a mother."

Olivia was early delivering. Her eyes lit wide with hope, she grabbed her Momma's hand and wouldn't let go, "Pray, Momma, pray." But Becka couldn't stop crying long enough to say one single word to Jesus. Crying because the feeling of being a mother after three years rushed in on her all at once; crying for all the tears Olivia couldn't shed herself. The women smacked the baby on the behind and it wailed nicely.

"Hell, naw!" Olivia spat venom when the women tried to take the baby off to get cleaned and wrapped up. The women turned back with the baby, so Olivia could see what she and her Daddy had created. Straightaway, the life seeped from Olivia's small frame. The infant looked healthy, but only time would tell.

The women exhaled and turned back to get the baby cleaned, but Becka stopped them this time. Two days later, Becka wrapped the stillborn in the pretty blue quilt Olivia had scrapped together. She laid her in the box with her Momma.

The elders say, "Naw, she just be a grandma."

Lawd Have Mercy

My destiny is tied to my skirt, so daily it flows with breezy blessings from above; sticks tight to my thighs revealing my desires for highs, when I'm feeling low; and pencils in my agenda for meetings that take me places, I never knew a hemline could go.

All black everything is the uniform I love. It is good for the form, but even more so the forum of how I am set up. Deep hued, ample hipped, big lipped, nappy naturally coiled, I smell like raw sugar, shea butter and virgin African soil.

I am owed recompense for my work, do well. Welled up in my throat, until I choke on the lies spewed right in my eyes, when they know, I am the cord that ties all things to life. Gone make me change my skirt?

Layers of fabric covering skinned knees, bruised shins, ashy thighs, connected to brittle hips broken in by age and the weight of chains. But my skirt, like my story, like my song is beauty - full of glory.

Even those that despise let compliments tumble, stumble from gripped lips and jealous eyes set with gangrene. My skirt may change, but the fact remains, that I Am the creator, designer, originator of dress. So, address me by my name, *Lawd have mercy*; I Am Goddess.

All that Glitters

Parker felt numb. The distance between her bed and the door appeared monumental. She turned her head to the right and looked downward to purvey the space between herself and the floor – that too was dangerously far. Time passed like pages turning with things to do, left undone; and people to see, left unseen; however, the thoughts paused, were reread, rehearsed, highlighted, and translated into foreign tongues. So, Parker sunk back into the covers and allowed the thoughts to continue their assault on her mind, body and spirit.

Tomorrow was her ally, no matter how unreliable. It would show up sure as day, but somehow Parker still felt forced to do all the planning, put in all the effort, make all the moves – big and small. What exactly was it good for, again? *Today* was an arrogant asshole – taunting, shaming, blaming, laughing hysterically. But, *Yesterday*, was always there to cuddle, "No my child, just think, lay back and reminisce on days passed." So, that's what she did as the yesterdays piled up; the tomorrows got fewer; and today began ignoring her existence.

A friend to talk to, a business meeting…an event would help. Parker patted the clouds of covers and puffs of pillows around her in search of her phone. She reached between the intricate layers to extract it from its burrow. Parker scrolled through her social media. She hadn't posted for over a month; but she had thousands of messages, comments, updates, invites and tags. She felt her heart's pace quicken and intentionally, meticulously logged out of each app. She checked her missed calls, saw she had numerous voice messages that she couldn't bring herself to listen to, and checked her text messages – there was a red-carpet event tonight.

Parker only needed to make two calls; one to her assistant apologizing for firing him and one to her agent telling him she was back open for business. Show business. Parker felt her body shift swiftly, her legs leveled down to the floor and she was up stretching. But then *Today* laughed, "Um, you haven't actually moved." She picked up the phone and placed the two calls. The buzz of the door startled her. She reached over and grabbed the gadget that showed who was at the door and electronically unlocked it. How did Tony get here so quickly? She looked at the time and two hours had passed; she must have dozed off again. Parker didn't know why she felt so embarrassed. They had been through this routine so many times before.

"Oh, my goodness!" Tony shouted in the hopes that Parker could hear him from behind the closed door with the shower running. "I don't know how one person can achieve a monumental mess in such a short time." Tony donned a mask, gloves and carried two trash bags. He began shoveling clothes – dirty, clean and with tags into one and food containers, papers, tissues, cardboard packaging and pill and wine bottles into another. He tried not to throw away any good merch or necessary papers, but he vowed long ago to never go through this dump meticulously again. Parker didn't deserve it.

She stood at the sink listening to the water in the shower run. She knew the sooner she got in, the sooner it would be over, and she would have to come out and face life – currently in the form of her assistant, Tony. Parker sat on the toilet and rested. The banging at the door startled her, and she jumped up and hopped in the shower allowing the water to engulf her body in the hopes that her mind, body and spirit would be renewed.

Parker emerged robed and refreshed. She barely recognized her bedroom. She noted to herself that she had better quit firing Tony because he may not come back again.

"You do know I had a good mind not to come back!?!" Tony was still shouting at the same decibel as when she was in the shower. "That last stunt you pulled was unforgiveable." Parker wasn't quite sure which last stunt was the last stunt he was referring to, so she remained quiet and contemplated. *Was it "accidently" locking her two toddlers outside by the pool, while she slept on the couch? Was it leaking the "story" that her husband was sleeping with the nanny, when he really only left and took the children for the sake of their safety? Was it berating and firing Tony for being a traitor, when he continued assist the man who was divorcing her by helping him get situated in a place with the kids she had neglected?*

The door buzzer saved her from having to make a guestimate. Parker checked the camera. It was hair and makeup; she buzzed them in. Less than an hour later, Parker was spackled and primped to perfection and unrecognizable, just like her bedroom. She hopped in the limo, and listened to her agent, Carl, on speaker. "Just tell them how excited you are to be returning for the new season of 'Hope in Hand,'" he instructed.

"Hope in Hand?" Parker questioned. Was she losing her mind, or was he? "I thought we went over this, *Carl*." Parker shook her head demonstratively, as if he could see her, "I no longer want to be a part of that show. I am not returning!"

Carl took a deep breath and spoke in a monotone to bring her back down to reality, "Look, Hope, that check is the only thing you have in hand. Remember, you are *nouveau riche*, and until you have some new offers come in, you'd be a fool to walk away from your livelihood. Especially, now that your husband is taking half."

"Well, isn't that what I pay you for? You can't tell me that no one has reached out to you about *me*? I'm a star, I'm Parker MFN Summers!" she snapped back.

"Right. And *Nobody* wants to work with Parker MFN Summers," Tony and Carl, rebutted in unison with clear disdain. This time it was Parker's turn to take a deep breath. This was her first attempt at facing life in a long time, and Frick and Frack were kicking her ass like she stole something. She remembered why she fired people. "Okay, but this is my final season. Clearly, I need you guys help," Parker spoke gently into the phone and glanced over at Tony in acknowledgement.

"You need professional help!" They shouted in unison loud enough for the driver to check his rear-view mirror. "Do you still have that number to the Psychologist I gave you?" Carl continued.

"Got it right here," Tony responded like the question had been directed at him, while pushing his phone into Parker's view. "It's on speed dial."

Parker acquiesced to Frick *and* Frack and reconciled in her mind to act her way through the rest of the evening. She took pictures smiling and laughing with her co-stars; stated with tears in her eyes that she was working on forgiveness in reference to her marriage; and eluded to taking time away from the spotlight because her girls needed her home. The night was a PR success and more importantly, she looked stunning in all the photos and footage.

Miles away and generations apart, Anisa, scrolled through social media and saw the flawless starlet, Parker Summers, in her feed. She was excited to see the cast of her favorite show in real life, just hanging out together. Anisa, couldn't help but feel for Parker and what she was going through with her cheating husband. But unlike many, Parker was giving her marriage her all for the sake of her children. If only she had those type of friends, strength, beauty, hell, that type of mother, her life could be so different. Anisa went to her favorite actress's page and scrolled through the pictures of her immaculate home and said a final prayer to restore her happy family. Anisa had lost all hope for herself. Her yesterdays were empty; her tomorrows promised nothing; so, today she released her existence.

Can I Get a Me Too?

Boys to Men is the natural progression
But boys are often halted in the procession
By transgressions not to be mentioned
Or they too become suspect in the decision
Never made by judge or jury
No one hears the case, much less the story
Shh, there's a hush over the village
Especially, when women perpetrate the rape and the pillage
Babysitters, Teachers, Mom's Best Friends Too
Commit crimes, called acts of kindness
Against children, called tutored youth

Can I get a me too?

But the expectation is protection for girls
From erections toyed with since adolescence
On boys too emotionally scarred to become men
And coached to refer to their trauma as good game
Women so willing to share wisdom now embody the victim
The criminal mind is disturbed, confused, locked up, but…
His corrupted innocence wasn't recounted by law or opinion
Violations against boys are victimless crimes
Rape culture good times
Maybe if we lock up the whole shrew slew
He could better empathize

#MeToo

Shake

Lynette woke to the bed shifting, artwork crashing to the floor, and the top of her dresser being cleared in one fell swoop. *Earthquake.* After the tremble, Lynette reached for the phone to call her mother.

"Oh, Sweetheart, are you okay?" her mother started before Lynette could say a word.

"Yes, mom, I'm fine. I was just checking on you," Lynette responded with relief. "I'll call you back."

At that moment Lynette's husband, Tom, was walking through the bedroom door with his thumbs up, "The kids and the dog are okay. Unfortunately, that feline survived too." Lynette thought the word feline was flattering and wasn't sure why Tom used the term as an insult.

"Oh, good." Lynette was already up and into her slippers. She picked up the salvageable items and put the rest in the trash. She hummed her way through all the damage in the rest of the house. After she was done, she swooshed her hands back and forth and smiled "light work."

Lynette knew Tom wanted to move back to the Midwest where he was from and where they had met in college. The wildfires were terrifying, the cost of living horrifying, and their house was dangling from a cliff, the view was to die for, literally. Every year engineers reinforced where they could, but warned that they should probably consider moving.

But Lynette loved the weather, the kids loved their school and her mother was just a short distance away in the Valley.

Her mother wouldn't survive the brisk winters of Illinois. So, Lynette lived her life constantly campaigning for California. *Can you believe this weather? 70 degrees and its February! Did I tell you that Ava DuVernay is visiting the girls' school? You know she directed the movies "Selma" and "Middle of Nowhere". That just doesn't happen in the middle of nowhere. Ahhhahaha. Tom, taste this. Straight from our garden; this is Eden. I'm going to walk the dog; he loves the hills. And look at my calves, I didn't think my legs or butt could get much better. Boom!*

Tom thought his marketing agency should hire Lynette for their next big commercial campaign. But beyond that her words were empty promises that lead to more tremors, broken glass, an unaffordable cost of living, shallow people, forest fires and a house teetering on the edge of destruction. Tom had a reoccurring bad dream of the engineer knocking on the door. *I'm sorry, Sir, this house is no longer safe to inhabit. It could topple off the cliff at any ti… AAAHHHH!* Tom woke abruptly from his fall.

Decidedly annoyed by Tom's worrisome tendencies and whining, the feline walked out the doggie door and into the Garden of Eden. She licked her paws and scratched at the earth. *Won't be long 'til your dream comes true.*

The Unloved

Undying love is uneventful. I rather push love to the edge and watch it teeter. Will it catch its balance like reciprocated romance that gives and takes in time and meter? Or will it plummet to its death? Even the wind withdrawals to watch its fateful splat. *Breathe.* Oh, you can't. Bleeding hearts lay bare for vultures to sup. I forget to ask about your existence because honestly I'm hoping you're secretive about your past hurts, protective of your impending emotions and in control of your feelings because not feeling is always a better/neater option. Let's laugh hard, lust loud, and sit quietly until we can't see pass each other. That's when I will know love has won, undying and uneventful – balanced with a book on its head. I'll run the sweeper while you're watching the game, and neither one of us will notice.

Unconditional love is non-existent love for people too stupid to leave. You hold on for dear life to a carcass amassed with fleas. What if I told you the only people to live happily ever after are those with shortened life spans due to STD's known curable. I want conditional love that could end with a weatherman's prediction: 30% chance of sprinkles. I'm sorry this isn't going to work, unless you lay your trench coat down in puddles before me; unless your umbrella is big and unbreakable against torrential rains that rage through the night; unless you can condition me to see rain as a game to be played and not abandoned for joy in the sun. Nah, I'm going to befriend a meteorologist who reminds me daily that picnics are based on conditions.

Unrequited love is my specialty. I like my intimacy with strings, ribbons, bells and baubles attached. But alas while

I'm planning futures and picking china, you're steady tapping my gullible behind. It's not that serious. Relax. Chill. And I can't resist because I'm the girl who loves quiet reservation, who sees cold sterility as a skill, who expects you to leave when the clouds don't disburse by noon. Don't ask, don't tell – until I implode with reasons why you should love me – reasons misunderstood by people not accustomed to sharing. I want to weather sunny days and delight in stormy fights full of insightful wisdom as to why you can no longer ignore our forever love story. *I shall not be moved.* At least, not until the pasty man in plaid pants reports: Spring is in the Air.

You Cannot Escape It

Jeremy's shoes were canvas, so even though he tried hard to avoid the melted snow on the way to school, water still seeped through. School was an escape from home and home was an escape from school. Home was a mess. Jeremy's Mom didn't have the energy to keep up, and she had even less energy to keep after the kids to keep up. So, it was a free for all of dirty dishes, piles of clothes everywhere but in the closet, and papers, magazines and books strewn across surfaces unseen and unknown. They would have gotten used to it, settled in good if it weren't for the occasional knock on the door that threatened to reveal their dirty secret; and the mice that mocked, "Ya'll need to do better."

School was a welcome respite. Jerry was the star of the football team, very popular with the ladies, and extremely intelligent. Jerry thought he was smarter than all his peers and most of his teachers, so he was always up for a debate. As his teachers became more and more frustrated trying to get back on task, they would always give in, give up or just plain give out. After a verbal bout with Jerry, Mr. Sanders went on leave never to return. It was rumored he had a stroke. Whenever a teacher was at their wits end the class would erupt, "Jeeerrrryy!" high fiving each other all around.

Jerry did genuinely believe he was smarter than everyone else, but on most days, he also felt they were just plain stupid; dull. He was a big fish in a small pond and he welcomed the bell's release at the end of each day. Today the school had a stench worse than usual. It always smelled to Jerry – stale people, stale air, and stale lessons. But today, the air made him angry. When he got to Mrs. Renner's class, he challenged her on her first statement and wouldn't let up until she left out the room in tears; in gym he clotheslined a kid for no reason; and at lunch he threw his whole tray of food away right after punching in his free lunch number. "This food's disgusting. Ew, I can't take the smell of this place!" he lashed out to anyone within earshot. No one disciplined Jerry because he was the star of the only thing the small town had going for it.

The last bell rang and Jerry was looking forward to fresh air and walking the new girl, Lisa, home. She was pretty enough, and he wanted to be the one to hit the school's newest target first. Jerry allowed his feet to get wet and watched the white gusts of air as he exhaled in and out. The smell was almost gone. They talked about where she was from and whether or not she liked Ohio. Jerry's hoodie proved thin and the cold air became less welcoming. He shoved his hands down in his jean pockets and felt something… fuzzy? The texture reminded him of something. He turned to Lisa and apologized, "My bad, I just remembered something. I have to go." Jeremy ran the whole 2 ½ miles home with the stench, the shock of humility, and the dead mouse still in his pocket.

The Stay

I own a timeshare in the depths of despair. I visited recently, not much had changed; same dreary curtains, dusty furniture, and dank smell. It took me days/weeks/months to find the doorway, so I stayed. Thank God, I stayed. The only other exit is to jump, OD, or shoot my way out, so I made the most of it. I caught up with, *why me*? We discussed my weight, finances, and relationships. Why me, couldn't stop laughing, when I brought up relationships.

On better days, I looked out the window. No, I couldn't see outside. The panes were boarded, but it's the effort that counts, right? The boards reminded me that there were blocks in my life; it wasn't all my fault. But after a while, the obstacles began resembling abstract art. I wasn't sure if I should cry or sip wine. Then I remembered, I'm an alcoholic and crying mandated feeling. At this particular resort, feeling is the last thing you want to do because every emotion ends in regret.

I moved away from the window and took to the bed. Ah, at last, my favorite vacation pastime; sleep. I could have slept the entire time and called it a blast with pictures to prove it. But in what should have been a stagnate state, the dreams began creeping in, each more frightening than the last; then the knawing thoughts of shouldn't I be doing something, anything; and worse than any of that, abruptly waking to the instinctive ideation that I do not belong here. I should jump, OD, shoot my way out...

I did my best to make sure the people around me were oblivious to my demise. Nevertheless, the incessant requests to behave normally, right in the midst of me working so diligently to remain amongst the living grew tiresome. But I couldn't tell my reasons for living that as of late, they weren't quite cutting it. So, after each brief "social" interaction, I retreated back to the villa of despondency, while remaining on call to behave humanlike when needed.

I've been visiting this same place once or twice a year, since I was a teen. Sometimes it is just a quick jaunt; in and out. Other times an extended stay. But this last sabbatical came out of nowhere. Life was good. I was awake and present. Peace gave way to enthusiasm. I made it! I had tools to keep me on a spiritual journey of enlightenment and purpose. Then the call came to confirm my reservation to Hotel Prospect Death. I clicked it straight to voicemail. Must be a mistake. I declined the invite.

In my earnest effort to avoid the trip, a week or more had passed, before I realized I had arrived, unpacked, and was already reacquainting myself with the staff. The staff were all in my head. They were laughing at my naiveté for believing I was free and high fiving my mind for playing such a great trick. Who trusts mental illness? Who in their right mind trusts a mind that is consistently wrong?

I pray I will never be stunned again by these getaways. As traumatizing as they can be, they are a sort of sanctuary for me when I overdo it or start to believe I can live like everybody else. It's like hitting the reset button before things go too awry. All I have to remember is *stay*. Thank God, I stay. Please, don't you leave us; just stay.

Masterpiece

Zion woke to a ray of light so bright, he knew his kin had come to remind him of who he was. A yawn and a stretch were enough to send the energy surging through his veins, up his spine and set his genius afire. He didn't have to go far – two steps in the efficiency apartment over to his easel, where his masterpiece patiently waited to rekindle the magic of the past three weeks. Would she be the one he wouldn't let go?

Zion picked up his brush and dipped it into the light that woke him from his lucid dream. Each stroke told a story, so far removed from the realm of reality that all who witnessed his work, recalled their own before birth. That is why people paid, bartered, sold to own just a piece of his perception of life. It was a slice of the promise, and each one thanked God for the chance to glimpse the divine. It was freely given, but somehow that got lost in the marketplace and *SOLD! to the highest bidder.*

Zion remained true to the vision and is visited by the Son every morning; kissed by the ancestors at dawn; and reminded to tell the masses, it will be all over in the morning. After completion, Zion decided he would not keep the masterpiece as a possession, just as the ones before and the ones to come. Never coveting anything or anybody; and never tying himself to this world's gratifications, greed, or gravity, Zion resides in Heaven and only visits us, here on Earth.

Bookshelf

I read my favorite book
Every now and then
At the end, I give a sigh of relief –
Yes, it is over. Finished. Done.
Yet close by whenever I reach

The Girl in the Window

Kendall looked out the window onto the bustling street below. Children were playing, cars were booming bass, and busses were hustling passengers to and fro. Kendall grabbed her coat and scarf from the hook. Her hat was neatly tucked inside the sleeves, and her matching gloves were in the coat pocket awaiting her entry. Once bundled from head to foot; boots and toed, striped socks included, Kendall walked back to the window, watched and waited.

The children outside were building a snowman. One kid tired of that and began throwing snowballs. A full snow brawl broke out and even passersby dipped, dodged and occasionally joined the fun. The Johnson siblings were the biggest group, and once their mom yelled for them to get inside and take off all those wet clothes, things quieted.

Kendall was hot in all her outer gear and had been perspiring profusely for the last hour. But there was still one kid outside kicking through snowdrifts, creating snow angels, and eating snow cupped in his mittened hands. Kendall cracked the window and called out to her little brother down below, "Hey, you!" Ryan looked up to see the ghost in the window.

That's what all the kids on their block called her. But Ryan was excited to see his sister, and he rushed up the front stoop and into the house. He was panting hard removing wet boots, mittens, hat and coat. He left them by the front door because he wasn't tall enough to reach the hooks. Ryan could hear the Johnson's as he ran pass the living room, up the stairs and to his sister's door.

Ryan knocked too loudly for Kendall's comfort. "Come in, Ryan," she whispered. Kendall knew her little brother might get in trouble for hanging out with her, but she missed him so very much. And he had been outside for hours without food, water or warmth.

"Kendall, Kendall! You came back!" The tears streamed down Ryan's face, and Kendall held him tight and rocked him back and forth in her arms.

"Shhh, you don't want the Johnson's to hear you, do you?"

Ryan didn't really care about the Johnson's. They were nice enough, but so many families had moved in and out, he had lost count. As soon as he got attached to one of the kids, they would abruptly up and leave. "No, but I thought you'd never return. They said you were gone forever."

"Isn't that what they always say? You know I would never leave you. I'm always here, even when you don't see me."

Her words put Ryan at ease. They sat on the floor and played cards. Match, war and speed were their favorites. After a while, Ryan grew tired of playing cards, and the air from outside and sitting still finally penetrated his being and chilled his core. Ryan coughed and looked over at the window.

"Kendall, you forgot to shut the window. It's cold in here." Ryan walked over and jumped as high as he could to reach the windowsill. But it was too high. He climbed on the bed and leaned forward as far as he could to connect his small frame and short arms with the ledge. But it was too far. "Kendall, help me. Help me!" He called loudly to his sister, but she had fallen asleep.

Ryan jumped down off his sister's bed and walked over to the fireplace. It was an old brownstone, so there was one on every floor. Kendall got the room with the fireplace because their parents said she was more responsible. As soon as Ryan lit the match, he remembered his mother and father's words, *Ryan, we told you not to play with matches. Do you want to burn the whole house down?* But once again, he remembered too late, and the friendly dancing flames were now feverishly out of control.

Ryan shook Kendall awoke, and the look of terror on her face chilled his soul. He was going to save her, and his parents and the dog, but instead he ran outside and played in the snow.

A Prostitute's Prayer
Chapter One Book Excerpt

Demonte breathed in and out through his mouth in anticipation, watching the white puffs of air. The bench he sat on was cold and firm on his tail-bone. He sat on the very edge so not to soil his green and white running suit on gum, bird excrement, and general grime. More than once the thought of jumping up, catching and then passing the other joggers entered his mind. That would warm him up. Again, he glimpsed at his phone. 7:22 AM. It was getting late. A lady emerged from around the curve and took multiple fast paced steps in rapid succession; however, her legs were so short and tightly wound that she barely made any ground. Another jogger appeared and easily overtook her penguin-like pace. 7:28 AM. Two more minutes and Demonte would have reluctantly or gratefully joined the strangers in the morning air in their morning routine.

Keelan rounded the bend just as Demonte turned for the final time to look at the bush that curtained each newcomer. He stood and grabbed Keelan by the neck. Keelan's eyes widened in impending doom; he knew that he was no match for Demonte, especially since his skill and strength were heightened by fury. The first punch landed between his eyes. His head hit the running trail hard. Demonte lifted his right tennis shoe high in the air and stomped down on Keelan's head. A woman entering the clearing screamed, almost tripping over the young man being stomped to death. She turned and ran back in the other direction. The next jogger, a man, slipped on the blood that now painted red the once grey passage way. He stayed down and crawled to the other side like a child who covers their own face thinking themselves now invisible.

The gore that hung onto his right leg unmercifully soaking his once pristine pants, socks, and now squishy shoes was now too much for even Demonte. He gave Keelan a swift kick in the stomach with his left foot. His body jerked in response. Demonte pulled out a gun and shot four times taking Keelan out of his misery. He laid the gun in plain view beside the dead body. Covered in Keelan's blood, Demonte again sat on the edge of the bench careful not to soil his suit any more than it already was. 7:35 AM. Demonte breathed in and out through his mouth in resignation, watching the puffs of white air.

"Forgive me Father for I have sinned," Demonte words held no remorse.

The whole city was in shock. The police, who first arrived at the scene, looked at the body that lay unrecognizable then at Demonte. Then back at the body, then back at Demonte. Finally, Demonte thrust his arms out straight, both ending in clenched fists, locked side by side. "I killed him." It was an open and shut case—the body, multiple eye-witnesses, the weapon, and a confession. But still the whole city stood as one unit in total mortified shock wrapped in disbelief. No one could believe that Demonte Aaron Davis was capable of doing such a thing. And the few people who had no idea who he was, were mortified by the brutal and brazen manner in which the crime was committed.

The next day the headlines read, "Superstar Athlete Murders Classmate", "NBA Bound, Now Prison Bound on Murder

Charges", "Inner City Hope Kills Chances," "From H.S. Honor Roll to Prison with No Parole."

A Prostitute's Prayer
Chapter Two Book Excerpt

Marissa stepped into the tunnel that transported her from first class global jet-setter to around the way hood rat. When she entered the airport terminal the media rushed her. "What do you have to say about Demonte?" "Why did he do it?"

"What?" she retorted in confusion and dismay. "My baby just died." For the first time since she had gotten the news, the tears streamed.

"Get the hell out of the way!" Rick's voice boomed over all the raucous. Give the lady a chance." The reporters eased back, not because of Rick, but because of the realization that she didn't *know*.

Marissa fell into Ricks arms and buried her face in his chest. She cried, "I lost my baby. I lost my baby, Rick. Rick, our baby…" He held her tight and nestled his head in the nape of her neck. He would have communed with her in her sadness, if the over abiding fear of telling her she had lost two babies hadn't annihilated all other emotion.

"Come sit down." Rick gently guided Marisa to a seat.

"No Rick, I want to get out of here. Get me out of here. Those reporters had the nerve to bring up, Demonte." Rick sat, and pulled Marisa down in the seat next to him. The reporters were waiting like vultures. He knew there was no way to get her out of there without them pouncing on her once again. He couldn't let her find out about her son that way and was almost grateful for the small amount of clearance the press was giving them now.

Rick took a deep breath that was so big it was unnatural, and he still could neither breathe nor speak. So, he took another one—equally as big and as awkward. "I have to tell you something first. It's about Demonte."

Marisa jerked her hands away in anger. "Demonte! Our baby, *Leanna* is gone." The look in Rick's eyes quieted Marisa's rage. "Oh God, what happened to Demonte?"

"He's fine." Rick corrected himself, "He's alive. But he's been arrested…for murder." Marissa slumped over in her seat. She had come home to bury her youngest, purely innocent daughter and found out her perfect superstar athlete son was a killer.

Rick was almost glad at her reaction. The media looked on in sympathy. And if that wasn't enough to make them retreat, the sight of Rula in his saggin' jeans and gang banga colors was enough to make them run. Rula had the most menacing face one could have and still be certifiably fine. His complexion was golden, and a ring of dark brown highlighted his pupils of the same golden bronze hue. He wore his hair in long braids that hung well below his shoulders, and he had a three-karat diamond earring in his left ear. He glared at the reporters one by one, and slowly placed his hand where his gun would have been if he weren't in the airport. Finally, for the hold-outs he revealed his diamond laden grille in a grimace, the letters K. I. L. L. glimmered in platinum. All on looking ceased.

"Come on, Marissa." He said his mother's name in one syllable. When she didn't respond, he tapped her shoulder. "Ma. Les' go." Marissa looked up and saw her youngest son. She grabbed his hand grateful that he was still alive and free. However ironic that was. He turned to look at his father. "I put the bags in the car. Les' go." Rick and Marissa got up like dutiful children, and Rula led them out of the airport to the car.

Rick held the door for Marissa, and they both climbed in the back of the Cadillac. "Ms. M" Steady's greeting said glad to see you, sorry for your loss, and you still looking good, with one head nod. Marissa hadn't spoken since she heard about Demonte, and still she couldn't find any words. She looked at Rula's best friend and tilted her head sideways in response. Steady passed a bottle of 151 to the back seat. "Or, you want E. and J." They always went old school to commiserate mourning – which was frequent.

Steady rolled weed in papers, and they bumped Tupac's *God Bless the Dead* on blast.
Simultaneously, Rick and Marissa were transported back into the present. "Would you please turn that hell down?" They got some semblance of relief when Rula turned the volume from 50 down to 45.

Marissa pressed hard on the automatic window and released the cloud of smoke. "Kids," she mumbled half under her breath. But she and Rick felt the sting of her word. It would never have the same meaning. Rick squeezed her hand and thought about how he had failed both his children. As if by osmosis, Marissa sat back and thought about how she had failed all five of hers. And they took a swig of the 151 and E.

and J., respectively.

A Prostitute's Prayer
Chapter Three Book Excerpt

The house stood crooked, cracked and beaten. The once golden color had now faded to a bereaved shade of yellowish beige. The white trim was washed in dirt and peeling pathetically. Marissa could not remember the last time she had actually slept in that house. When she came to town she always stayed in the best hotels, downtown penthouses or guest quarters owned by her acquaintances. Just a couple days ago she was in Puerto Vallarta lying on a private beach with her lover sipping mimosas outside of his villa. Now she was in Columbus, Ohio drinking the contents of a brown paper bag at 112 E. 22nd and back on Section 8.

The music assaulted her ears from the street, and her eyes glazed over as she witnessed all of the cars, trucks, motor cycles, bikes, and big wheels strewn across the lawn, drive, and on the curb. They were 'nouveau riche' in transportation. Marissa hesitated to go up the steps. Rick held her arms and slightly pushed her to keep it moving. The sooner he could get her in a room and to a bed the better. He did not want her falling out or crying uncontrollably. Nobody needed that kind of drama, especially from her.

"Grandma!"

"Mamaw!"

Marissa's grandchildren greeted her at the door. "Oh, babies Grandma miss you." Rick took the bottle. And Marissa squatted down and hugged all three of them at once. They were her oldest daughter, Kim's children. Devin was 8, Devonte was 7, and Denisha was 4. She held them close; eyes shut tightly and tried to forget. She felt a tap, tap on her left shoulder. When she opened her eyes, she saw Lil' Ricky. He was three-years-old and his hair was in long braids, and he had a big diamond earring in his left ear. "Oh, Baby...I almost didn't see you. You have gotten to be such a big boy." Marissa hadn't seen him in a while because his mother kept him away when she was mad at Rula, which was most of the time.

Lil' Ricky grinned and nodded his head, "I Bi' Boy."

Marissa felt her legs start to cramp. "Wait babies give grandma a chance." She looked over at the big leather sectional and saw Lil' Ricky's mama, Peaches, sitting there like she owned the place. She couldn't stand her. Rula was 15 and she was 19, when she got pregnant. But it wasn't rape in nobody's mind but hers. When she threatened to call the police, Rula had cussed her out so bad saying, *at least she's going to be a mother to her child, instead of some high price hoe*, that she hung up the phone and cried herself to sleep in her suite at the Renaissance. She wished she was there right now.

"Hi Peaches." The girl just rolled her eyes. Rula's other baby mama, Sophia, walked in the room as Marissa spoke. She was carrying their eight-month-old son, whose name was Rick too. But they called him Lil' Rul. "Oh, Sophia please let me hold the baby."

"Yes, Ma'am," she replied and gave her the boy. All the grandkids gathered around Marissa.

"Mamaw, where's Leanna? Did you bring her home wit' you?" Denisha asked sadly. Marissa bit her lip, and her eyes wandered about for help.

"Grandma, did you bring presents?" Devonte jumped in before Marissa could speak.

"I wanna dowl, I wanna dowl." Denisha bounced up and down forgetting her former question. Marissa always brought presents home to the children. But on this occasion, it hadn't even crossed her mind. *They* hadn't even crossed her mind, until she walked through the door.

She looked at their mothers. "We'll all have to go shopping. Sometime soon." All three of the women looked at her like she was speaking a different language. "All of us. *Please*." Marissa tried to look helpless. They frowned, smacked their lips, and rolled their eyes in response.

"Yeah, that's coo,'" Rula answered for them. And it was done.
Marissa looked back at Peaches. "*All* of the children."
Peaches had three other children by different men or *boys*, (Marissa wasn't sure). "I'm going to head upstairs. It's been a long day. Don't stay up too late…" realizing no one was listening she stopped talking and handed the baby back to Sophia.

Marissa stood up and walked over to her oldest son, Kevin, and squeezed his hand. He gave her a hug. Both of them were almost overcome by sadness, but Kevin quickly spoke to interrupt the oncoming emotions. "You staying here tonight, Marissa?"

"Of course," she responded matter of fact, like she had never stayed anywhere else.

"Well, I am going to head out. I'll be back in the morning." Kevin grabbed his coat. Kevin was the only one of her children that had moved out.

"O.K., we'll talk more tomorrow."

Marissa walked up to Demonte's room. Rick was sitting on the bed with his head down covered by his hands. He had brought her bags up upon realizing the grandkids were enough of a distraction to keep anyone from losing it in sadness or anger, at least for the time being. Rick got up as she entered. "Do you need me to get you anything?"

"No, I'm fine. You can take this liquor, too." She lifted the bottle from the dresser and took one more drink. "Here, thanks for everything."

"Do you need me to stay?" He tried to mask his desire to be around her, with genuine concern.

Marissa frowned and thought to herself. *Now why would I want that?* "No. Rick. Please. You have done so much. Go home and get some rest."

He kissed her forehead. "I'll call in the morning."

Marissa sat on the bed and looked about the room. Demonte's room was always immaculate. The bed was made with his two pillows covered by the comforter. He didn't want his pillows overexposed to the elements. A dresser stood on the right side of the bed and boasted one framed picture of Leanna and one of his niece and nephews, except for Lil' Rul who hadn't been born when the photograph was taken. All other personal items were neatly arranged in the two top drawers. Above the dresser mirror hung his plaques for everything from MVP of the basketball team to Best Dressed to Top Academic Achievement. There was a shelf with two trophies, the rest he kept packed away, and each had medals hanging from them. His closet door was shut, but she knew all his clothes were neatly organized by style and color, shoes lined up accordingly. On the left side of the bed there was a small table with a book, daily planner, and a lamp. There was a window on the adjacent wall that looked out onto the street. A chest of drawers was beside the window with a t.v. atop it. Three of Leanna's paintings hung on the wall one underneath the other. All the furniture matched. There was another large abstract piece above his bed that Leanna had presented to him one Christmas. Now, they were both gone.

Marissa slipped off her shoes and laid her head back on the pillow. "Lord, please here me. I know your word says you answer prayers, even a prostitute's prayer, Lord?" The tears flooded and her chest heaved. "I don't know what I've done." She sounded like a baby even to herself and tried to gain control. "Please, we need you, Lord. Tell my baby I love her. I love you, Leanna. Mommy loves you." Marissa cried herself to sleep.

Black Patients Matter

'All Patients Matter' aligns with 'All Lives Matter,' and instead of being a call to action, it is a call to complacency, while African American lives are lost and disregarded in our current healthcare system. So, in an effort to better African American patient outcomes, 'Black Lives, Patients and Doctors Matter' should always be the focus for positive change.

As an African American who is hyper aware that race matters in my life in general, but also through my lived experience of having a loved one who was a patient at a mental health facility, I know first-hand the severity of this issue. When my family member had a white case manager, she would sit in her office and pretend to listen, while the patient ranted nonsense. When family tried to discuss the situation with her, she blocked all efforts stating that her client was an adult, and she could not discuss the case. When she left the agency, and the client got a Black case manager, she came out to visit and speak with the family directly. She picked up the client from home, let them know she didn't want to hear all that and took the client to get Social Security Benefits; which were granted on the first attempt. The patient had a Black nurse, and one day she asked if the patient wanted to change doctors. She was asking, but all the while she was nodding her head in that knowing "Yes" manner. So, the patient was switched to a Black healthcare provider. I watched my family member go from walking around like a drooling zombie, to becoming a fully functioning young person who is no longer sleeping and staying isolated all day, but instead is social, working and saving to live independently. The first day, we saw the new Black doctor, he told the patient, "You are too young and have too much going for you to live like this." The same Black nurse worked with our family for over a year to get the patient's student loans forgiven due to the disability. I cannot begin to explain the difference it made in my loved one's progress, when we started thinking and acting on their behalf in terms of race.

Black patients need Black doctors. There are studies that show Black healthcare providers show the most empathy to all patients, regardless of their demographic. On the flip side, Black patients receive the least amount of empathy from healthcare providers who are not Black. African Americans face discriminatory practices that impair their quality of life and quite often result in the loss of life when both could be avoided with better diagnosis and treatment. Unfortunately, Black people also face discrimination when it comes to getting into the healthcare profession, for example, fewer African American students are accepted into medical school, and the racism continues once on the job. All these factors need to be addressed.

I have always sought out Black dentists, pediatricians and general practitioners, but I will admit that for some reason when it came to mental health for myself and my family, I oftentimes fell short. I currently see an African American Psychoanalyst and in all my years in and out of therapy, it is the first time that my diagnosis resonates; I can retain the information shared due to the trust factor built by actively being listened to; and I am optimistic about the progress I am making, not only mentally, but also socially, financially and across the board.

When seeking help, it is crucial that you remain vigilant in finding the best healthcare providers for you, specifically. African American people are the only people who consistently advocate for African Americans to receive better diagnosis, treatment and outcomes. 'Black Lives, Patients and Doctors Matter.'

Call to Action

"That's the Story of My Life," is a book of short stories that are great conversation starters for mental illness, mental wellness and all things in between. With suicide on the rise for African American Youth, Stephanie R. Bridges, believes it is crucial that we begin addressing mental health head on. Our youth need us more than ever, and our failure to address these issues is costing their lives. If you'd like to be a part of the conversation, please do the following:

1. Read the Book
2. Choose one or more stories that resonates with you
3. Create a video sharing why you think the book is important and relay your personal thoughts or story to our youth
4. Tag me in the post on Facebook, IG or Twitter https://www.facebook.com/stephanie.bridges.144 Instagram, https://www.instagram.com/stephanier.bridges/ or Twitter, https://twitter.com/i_spat
5. Use the Hashtag #ttsoml

Other Publications by this Author –

Children's Books:
"If I Were Part of the Animal Kingdom"
"My Favorite Color is Blue"
"Fight the Air Guy"
"Can We All Just Get Along"

Tween:
"Keep the Peace" Anthology
"Keep the Peace" Companion Journal

YA:
"That's the Story of My Life"

Adult Christian Poetry:
"I SPaT"

Non-Fiction:
"Seeking and Securing Individual Artist Grants and Other Funding"
"The Ten Tiny Steps Between You and Publishing Your Book"

About the Author

In this book Best-Selling Author, Stephanie R. Bridges, shares her lived experience with mental illness and alcoholism and drug addition through her fiction and creative non-fiction stories and characters. She is a spoken word artist, lyricist, author, publisher and entrepreneur. Stephanie lives in Columbus, Ohio, with her family and pets. She is a recovering alcoholic with twenty-seven years of sobriety, she graduated from The Ohio State University with a B.S. in Secondary English Education in 1993, and she started her publishing company, In Spirit Power and Truth Publishing (I SPaT), LLC in 2014. Stephanie would love to connect with you. She is Stephanie R. Bridges on all her social media. Be sure to check out https://www.stephanierbridges.com/ to learn about new releases and order her full catalog of publications. Also, if you are a published or aspiring author, join the Bridges Book Club at https://www.bridgesbookclub.com/ for assistance and support on your writing journey.